Nothing to CHEER About

by Marcie Anderson

Apple IIc is a trademark of
Apple Computer, Inc.

Cover photo by Bichsel Morris
Photographic Illustrators.

Published by Willowisp Press, Inc.
401 E. Wilson Bridge Road, Worthington, Ohio 43085

Printed in the United States of America
10 9 8 7 6 5 4 3

ISBN 0-87406-016-8

One

MY summer was ruined on May twenty-sixth. Scott saw the car pulling out of the driveway. But the driver didn't see us.

"Hang on, Charlie!" Scott yelled as he swerved his motorbike to miss the car. I tried to hold on to his waist. But it all happened too fast. Scott swerved sharply to the right and hit the curb. I flew off the back of the motorbike and crashed on my right leg.

"Scott! My ankle!" I yelled, bursting into tears. Nothing had ever hurt me that much. When Scott tried to help me sit up, I was sure a knife was stabbing me on the inside of my right ankle.

"No, don't touch me!" I screamed. I couldn't believe this was happening to me. I saw blood on Scott's arm. Someone took my helmet off.

"I'm so terribly sorry," the woman was saying. "I just didn't see you behind me. Oh, dear, let me go in and call your parents for you." Scott gave her the telephone numbers.

I curled up sobbing on the grass next to the street. Scott held my hand and kept saying, "It's all right. It's all right." But the pain in my ankle told me everything was not all right.

I cried even harder when I saw my mom. Her face was white and tense. "Charlie, Honey! You poor thing. Scott, just how did this happen?" she asked.

Mom and Scott helped me into the car. Scott sat with me in the backseat on the way to the hospital.

My mom was going on and on about how unsafe motorbikes are. I had had to convince my parents to let me ride with Scott on his new motorbike. Mom and Dad finally agreed, but only if we stayed in our neighborhood and didn't go on any main roads.

Scott sat crunched in the corner of the seat. He looked embarrassed.

"Mom, please. It wasn't Scott's fault," I said.

"Well, maybe not," Mom said as she drove into the hospital emergency parking area. "But your motorbike-riding days are over, Charlie."

A man in a white uniform brought a wheelchair and helped me into the emergency room. My ankle was already swelling above my running shoe. Every time I moved my leg the pain in my ankle made me start crying again.

Mom began filling out some yellow hospital

forms. Scott sat down next to my wheelchair and held my hand. We could hear a little boy crying in another room. A woman sitting across from us was holding an ice pack on her arm. Hospital workers were hurrying back and forth.

"Can't they hurry up, Mom?" I asked. "My ankle is killing me."

Just then Scott's parents arrived. I'd never met Mr. and Mrs. Gibson before. Scott and I had only known each other for six weeks. We met at a party his cousin Lisa gave. She's also my best friend. We both made varsity cheerleading for next year in ninth grade.

Scott is older, sixteen and in tenth grade at the high school. My parents wouldn't let me date yet. But Scott came over to my house once or twice every weekend and we met at parties. My parents let me meet him at the movies sometimes. And we talked on the phone every day.

Now I had to meet his mom and dad with my hair all messed up and my eye makeup running from crying so much. It wasn't the best way to meet such a neat guy's parents, I thought.

"We're so sorry about your leg, Charlie," his mom said. "Let's hope it's just a bad sprain."

Scott went off with his parents to fill out his own forms. His arm was cut, but it had stopped bleeding. His parents said they wanted a doctor to check him over to make sure he was all right.

Finally a nurse came up to us. "Charlene Hunter?" she asked.

"Charlie, please," I said. I was always embarrassed to be called by my full name. Scott didn't even know my name was really Charlene. I tried to keep that a secret when I could.

"Let's move you into the fracture room," the nurse said. "The doctor can check you over in there."

"Fracture? Mom, is my ankle broken? What about cheerleading?" I asked. Our whole squad was going to cheerleading camp for two weeks in June.

"We'll just have to wait and see, Charlie," Mom said.

Another man in a white uniform helped me onto a rolling cart. A nurse propped up my leg and put ice packs around my ankle. She put a thermometer in my mouth and took my blood pressure, too.

"Hello, I'm Dr. Fowser, the emergency room physician. I'll be checking you over, Charlie," she said. Dr. Fowser was a pleasant young woman with straight blonde hair. She gave me a complete exam. I was glad the emergency room had a woman doctor.

"Everything except your right ankle seems okay, Charlie. Let's get some X rays of that ankle. And we'll send for the orthopedic resident to check it out."

I was wheeled into the X-ray room. A young woman took X rays of the side, back and front of my ankle. I had to bite my lip when she moved my leg for the X rays. Didn't she know how much it hurt? I wondered.

I was taken back to the fracture room where my mom was waiting. A very handsome doctor came up to us.

"Geoffrey Baum," he said as he shook my hand. "I'm the ortho resident on duty. So you have an ankle I need to see?"

Dr. Baum wheeled me over to the wall and pulled a green curtain around my cart. He looked at the X rays of my ankle.

"Can my mom be here, please?" I asked in a tiny voice.

"Sure, I'll get her. She can help me, anyway," he said. "We're going to have to cut your jeans off to treat your ankle."

"WHAT?" I gasped. "These jeans cost forty dollars! And I paid for them with my own money from babysitting." I wasn't so afraid to speak up if he was going to ruin one of my best pairs of jeans.

"Well . . . we can't just pull them off because we might make your ankle worse," the doctor said. "I guess I can try to slit the seam on the injured leg with a scalpel. Then you could sew the seam back up. How would that be?"

So my mom helped Dr. Baum cut off my jeans. He gave me a hospital gown first to cover up myself.

As soon as he started touching my ankle I started crying again. He must have thought I was a little baby. I really couldn't help it though. I even screamed when he poked around at that little bump of bone on the inside of my ankle.

Dr. Baum patted my shoulder when he was finished. "Charlie, you have a displaced fracture-dislocation of the medial malleolus," he said. "That means that little bone at the side of your ankle is broken and pushed out of place."

I held my mom's hand tightly.

"The good news is that the circulation in your foot is okay. There doesn't seem to be any nerve or artery damage."

"But how soon can you fix it?" I asked. I couldn't help it. I started to cry again. "I . . . I'm going to cheerleading camp the last two weeks of June and . . ."

"No, sorry, no chance of that," Dr. Baum said and patted my knee. "We're taking you to surgery right away to fix that ankle. You'll still be in a cast at the end of June, Charlie."

Two

I cried all the way up to surgery . . . down the halls, past desks, up elevators. I couldn't stop.

Until now my fourteenth summer was going to be perfect. I had a cute, older boyfriend with a motorbike. Cheerleading camp was in June. Cheerleading practice was to be held every day in August. A camping trip was planned with Lisa and her parents. I even had a regular babysitting job lined up to earn money for new school clothes for ninth grade.

I'd worked hard and planned everything out. Lisa and I had spent hours on the phone talking about how much fun we'd have. And now everything was ruined by one stupid accident.

"Come on, Charlie. Crying won't make things any better," my mom said. She tried to be comforting. It didn't work.

I waited on my rolling cart while Mom filled out a hundred or so hospital forms. Nurses came to take blood, my temperature and tests. Finally they gave me some pain medication. By then I was sure my ankle would need amputation . . . at the knee.

"Mom, how about lunch?" I asked. I hadn't eaten since dinner the night before.

"Sorry, Honey. The nurse said you can't eat or drink anything since you're going into surgery right away," Mom said.

We waited and waited for the orthopedic surgeon to show up. My leg already felt like it was frozen solid, but the nurses kept bringing fresh ice packs.

About two o'clock my dad arrived. He'd been at his Saturday morning golf game and had just heard about my accident. Right behind Dad was Dr. Baum and the surgeon he worked for, Dr. Moyer.

Dad hugged me before they wheeled me into surgery. "Everything will be fine, Honey. Don't worry," he said.

How could I not worry? I wondered. A cheerleader with a broken leg has nothing to cheer about.

Making the varsity cheerleading squad for ninth grade was just about the best thing that ever happened to me. I was a basic klutz in elementary school. My parents finally started me on lessons to improve my coordination— ballet, tap, ice skating. By eighth grade I was pretty good at dance and movement. I exercised all year to build up my strength. I ran every day after school. And I practiced cheers with Lisa, since she was already a junior varsity cheerleader. The night before cheerleading tryouts, my parents heard me practicing in my sleep.

Two, four, six, eight,
Who do we . . . (mumble, mumble).

My original cheer for tryouts was one of the best. In fact the whole squad would be performing it at cheerleading camp in June. But I wouldn't be there with them, I remembered.

Tears were trickling down my face when the doctor told me to count backward. "Don't worry," Dr. Baum said. "We'll just make a small incision so we can fix that broken bone."

"Ten, nine, eight, seven, si . . . "

* * * * *

The recovery room was a blur. Nurses and doctors came and went. Dr. Baum asked me how I felt. My ankle still felt like a hive of bees had attacked. My head was throbbing. And I kept trying to throw up and couldn't.

A nurse gave me a shot and changed the liquid dripping into my hand through a needle. "That will help your nausea," she said.

After a while they took me to my room. My ankle was wrapped in a brown elastic bandage. The back of my ankle and calf were protected by a half cast. It didn't look too awful. I thought I could still get back in shape in time for cheerleading practice in August.

Dr. Moyer came in to see my parents. He patted my head and said something about my being a good sport. I was tuning in and out by then. ". . . open reduction internal fixation of right ankle . . . no complications . . . screw put in bone . . . cast the leg . . . crutches . . . " the doctor was saying.

By the next day I was totally tuned in. Dr. Baum came in to check on me.

"Won't I need to have a cast on my ankle?" I asked him.

"Right," he said. "Cast goes on tomorrow before you go home. Then we'll change the cast when we check your incision."

"But can't you take the cast off by June sixteenth?" I asked.

Dr. Baum sat down in the chair next to my bed. "Charlie, you've got to accept this injury. You broke a bone here. You can't go to cheerleading camp this year," he said.

"But what about cheerleading this fall?" I asked. "I worked so hard and I'm on the varsity." My voice trembled and so did my chin. I didn't want to cry in front of Dr. Baum again. Then I'd really be labeled "Cry baby!"

"We'll have to see about that this fall," he said. "Your ankle needs time to heal. And then you'll be out of shape by fall."

Well, that shows how much you know, Dr. Geoffrey Baum, I thought. I'm not going to get out of shape. I've worked too hard to become a cheerleader. A broken ankle isn't going to stop me.

As Dr. Baum left, a hospital volunteer brought in a little basket of pink roses with a pink get-well helium balloon floating above. The tiny card said, "SORRY about your ankle. Love, Scott."

What a sweetheart! I thought.

Scott came to visit that night with Lisa. They brought a big get-well card signed by all the cheerleaders.

"All the kids heard about your accident today in school," Lisa said. "Everyone was really upset, especially all the cheerleaders."

"What did Mrs. Mac say?" I asked. Mrs. MacIntosh is our cheerleading advisor.

"She said she'd talk to you later about camp. Oh, Charlie, I can't believe you have to miss it," Lisa said. "It won't be the same without you."

"I didn't want her to be gone all that time anyway," Scott said with his gentle, shy smile.

"Why don't you go say hi to my parents,

13

Lisa?" I asked. I gave her a knowing look. "They're in the coffee shop."

After Lisa left, Scott sat next to me on the bed. His arms went around me in a warm hug.

"Oh, Charlie, I never, ever meant for you to get hurt on my motorbike. Maybe I'll sell it."

"No, no, it wasn't your fault," I said. "Besides, you worked a long time to earn the money for it."

Scott moved back so his face was next to mine. "I'm so glad I met you, Charlie," he said. "You're the first girl I can really talk to." His lips brushed mine in a gentle kiss. "I'm just so sorry about your ankle. But don't worry. The summer won't be ruined, not for us." His arms went around me again.

And that's how we were when my parents and Lisa came back. Fortunately, they knocked before they came in.

Three

"GOOD morning, Charlie." Dr. Baum knocked and entered my room early on Tuesday morning. He really was the most handsome doctor. He looked like . . . like someone famous. Burt Reynolds? Yes. It must be his moustache, I thought.

"Let's take a look at that ankle and see if you're ready to go home," he said. Dr. Baum peeled off the elastic bandage covering my ankle.

I knew I was ready to go home. There was no doubt about it. After three days in the hospital, I was tired of doctors, nurses, ice packs, lukewarm food, visitors (except Scott), and bedpans! That was the worst of all. I couldn't wait to be up and walking around so I wouldn't get out of shape.

"Okay, the incision looks fine," Dr. Baum said. "Let's take you down to the fracture room and get a cast on."

Dr. Baum covered the bottom half of my leg

with some fiberglass goo that quickly dried into a cast. The top of the cast was just below my knee. My toes stuck out at the end of the cast.

"Now, you can't get this cast wet," the doctor said. "That includes swimming, of course, and no showers. You'll have to take sponge baths or let your leg hang out of the bathtub."

"No showers!" I said to myself. I took a shower every day at home so I could blow dry my hair before school. This broken ankle was making my life worse and worse.

"Don't put any weight on that ankle for the first ten days," he said, "not until we see you at our office. We'll send someone up soon from physical therapy to teach you how to use your crutches."

I'd rather you taught me, Dr. Baum, I thought.

"Now, keep your leg elevated and dry," the doctor said. "Wiggle your toes a lot to help the circulation."

"When will it stop hurting? And what about school?" I asked. I wished I had a photo of Dr. Baum to take back to school to show the cheerleaders.

"I'll give you a prescription for some pain medication to be taken as needed," he said. "And you can go back to school, oh, say next

Monday. Later, we'll talk about cheerleading."

What would that be like, I wondered . . . school on crutches. I'd never manage the school bus. Mom would just have to drive me. I'd have no gym class and no cheerleading practice. I couldn't even walk to get hamburgers after school. But at least everyone could sign my cast.

"Will you sign my cast, Dr. Baum?" I asked. I wanted to say, just sign it "Dr. Baum, Burt Reynolds' look-alike."

"Sure, here you go," he said as he signed my cast. "Just tell your friends they have to use felt-tip pens on this fiberglass cast." Some of the nurses signed my cast, too, so it didn't look so bare by the time I went home.

I was so happy to be home again! I practiced walking on my crutches most of the afternoon. Scott came over to see me after school. He couldn't stay long though, because he had to start studying for his final exams.

Wednesday night all the cheerleaders came over. They brought me a big bunch of helium balloons tied with ribbons.

There are six of us on next year's varsity cheerleading squad. Lisa is my best friend and she's also captain of the squad. Pam is another good friend. She's really pretty and athletic. She's a great swimmer, too, and is on the varsity swimming team. The others on the squad are Terri, Jill, and Karen.

We were all over the house that evening . . . my room for records and tapes, the kitchen for snacks, the family room for T.V. video games. Everyone was amazed at how well I could walk with my crutches. They all tried walking with them.

"Too bad we don't have six pairs," Pam said. "Then we could have a race."

"Charlie, you'd better slow down," my dad called out from the living room.

"I'm fine, Dad. Have to keep in shape," I called back. I even put a tiny bit of weight on the cast once or twice as I was using my crutches. But that hurt too much, so I stopped.

I took more pain medication at nine that night, right after my friends left. My ankle was hurting a lot by then. I laid on the couch in the family room and waited for Scott to call.

"Charlie, Scott's on the phone," my mom called from the kitchen.

I must have dozed off. I grabbed my crutches and hobbled into the kitchen to the phone. My ankle was worse, much worse.

"How's it going, Charlie? Do you feel better?" Scott's voice was soft.

"No, I feel worse. My ankle hurts as much now as any time since my operation," I grumbled.

Scott wasn't that sympathetic. He probably thought I was a baby.

By eleven that night I was fighting back tears. My ankle was burning, aching, hurting. My toes were numb.

"Mom, look! My toes are turning blue! Do something," I cried. My dad put his arms around me and patted my back. Mom went off to call the doctor.

We met Dr. Baum and Dr. Moyer in the emergency room at midnight. I had taken more pain medication, but it hadn't helped.

I was crying *again* by the time we saw the doctors. I wondered if Dr. Baum must think that's all I do.

Dr. Moyer looked at my foot and around the edges of my cast. "Swelling here, some loss of circulation to the foot," he said. "We'll have Dr. Baum bivalve your cast."

"Bivalve!" my mom cried, sounding hysterical. "What's that?"

"We'll just make a cut on each side of the cast," Dr. Moyer answered. "That will relieve the pain. You've been walking too much, Charlie."

I looked down, embarrassed.

"We'll wait a few days and then put on a new cast," Dr. Moyer went on. "For now you go home and keep that leg elevated. Stay sitting down unless you have to get up for something important, like going to the bathroom or going to bed."

I nodded meekly and went off with Dr. Baum to the fracture room.

He made a cut on each side of my cast with an electric saw. As soon as the cast was looser, my leg and ankle stopped hurting so much.

"You know, Charlie, a lot of your recovery depends on you," Dr. Baum said. "If you don't follow instructions, you could be in a cast for months. And your ankle might never heal properly."

"But I have to stay in shape! I have cheerleading this fall . . . " My voice trailed off as he shook his head.

"You've got to let this ankle heal," the doctor said firmly. "Or you might never be able to do anything athletic for the rest of your life. You could even have a permanent limp."

"But I will be able to go back to cheerleading in the fall, won't I?" I asked. I couldn't believe it. After everything I'd worked for, now this! It was bad enough to miss cheerleading camp. But I couldn't miss being a cheerleader for football and basketball, too.

"It might be best if you weren't a cheerleader this fall," Dr. Baum said. He started putting tape around the cuts on the cast. "Your leg will be out of shape and weak. You don't want to land on it wrong and rebreak your ankle."

"But I can't quit cheerleading!" I cried. My chin was starting to tremble. "It means everything to me. You don't know how important being a cheerleader is at my school." I guess I couldn't expect him to understand.

"I do understand, Charlie," he said. "I missed a whole season of wrestling in college because of surgery on my knee."

"But did you get back on your team the next year?" I asked.

"Yes, but it wasn't easy. I had to fight for it," he said.

Well, I could do better than that, I thought. I'd start fighting right away. I wasn't going to lose being a cheerleader and being part of the best group in junior high. And my future . . . I was counting on being a cheerleader in high school, too.

"You're all set, Charlie. Now stay off that ankle," Dr. Baum repeated. He put his hand on my shoulder. "Remember, your recovery depends on you. You can go back to school next week, but take it easy. Walk as little as possible. We'll see you this Saturday to check your incision and put on another cast."

"How long am I going to be stuck in a cast?" I asked.

"Oh, six or seven weeks. That depends on

how fast the break heals," he said.

"But that's till the middle of July!" I said.

Dr. Baum helped me up and handed me my crutches. "It's up to you, Charlie. If you're not careful you could be in a cast till fall."

Talk about a ruined summer, I thought . . . no cheerleading camp, no swimming, no camping trip, no motorbike rides, no ballet lessons and no babysitting. What was left?

Scott. At least I still had him.

Four

SO there I was sitting at home from Thursday till Monday. My friends will tell you I am not one to sit at home alone. Lisa brought all my books home for me. I had to start studying for finals anyway.

Mom took me to the doctors' office on Saturday morning. I didn't even get to see Dr. Baum again. Dr. Moyer put on my new cast.

My friend, Pam, was having a pool party on Sunday. And she had already invited Scott for me. At first Mom wanted me to miss the party. I had to promise I'd sit still at the party and not walk too much.

I had an awful time getting ready on Sunday afternoon. My mom had to help me take a bath, since I couldn't get in or out of the tub by myself. That stupid tub was so awkward. Mom had to wash my hair for me, too. I had to bend over the kitchen sink with my cast stuck out to the side. Nothing was easy with a cast on my leg.

Then I had to try to find something decent to wear to the party. Pants were out because they wouldn't fit over my cast. I tried on a sundress and then a skirt. They looked stupid with that white cast sticking out.

"Mom, can you help me find something to wear?" I called. I threw the sundress and skirt in the bottom of my closet.

"Nothing fits!" I yelled at Mom as she came into my room. It made me sick to think of all my nice summer clothes that I couldn't even wear.

We went through my closet and all my drawers. Finally we found some old baggy white shorts that would fit over my cast. It was a good thing Mom was with me because I lost my balance when I tried to pull the shorts on. Mom caught me just in time.

"Oh, great," I snapped. "Watch Charlie the Klutz break her other ankle." Mom just smiled and handed me my new striped top. At least that would still fit me. I put on one white loafer.

"Too bad I can't switch this cast for the other white shoe," I said, looking in my long mirror.

"Oh, Mom, look. My hair looks awful." I had had to dry it sitting down, so I couldn't see how it was turning out. "Maybe I can fix it with my curling iron."

Mom and I fussed with my hair till it was time to leave. But I never did get it looking just right. And I knew everyone would be looking at me because of my cast.

Dad took me to the party and helped me to Pam's pool deck. He put me in a padded lounge chair. Then he put on his stern face.

"Now, I want to see you still sitting there when I come back to pick you up," he said. "Have a good time. But don't get wet!"

Scott came to the party with Lisa because they lived near each other. All the cheerleaders were there, as were Pam's friends from the swim team. Everyone crowded around me and signed my cast.

Scott brought me some lemonade and sat down beside me. "Did you hear the good news?" he asked. He sounded excited. "I got a job for this summer at the community pool!"

"That's great, Scott," I said with little enthusiasm in my voice. He'd be at the pool all summer, watching cute girls in bikinis. And I couldn't get my leg wet or my cast would melt!

"I'm going to be a junior lifeguard," Scott said, "at the wading pool and helping in the big pool during the busy times. The swim coach at the high school helped me get the job."

"Oh, that's right," I remembered. "You said you were on your swim team in high school."

Swimming season was over before I met Scott. "Pam's a swimmer, too. Those guys over there are on her team." I pointed to Rusty and Jason on the other side of the pool.

"Hey, I've seen them at lots of our meets. I'd better go talk to them for a few minutes. You don't mind, do you?" he asked. Scott was gone before I could answer.

I hardly saw him again for the rest of the party. Well, I did *see* him. He swam races with Rusty, Jason, and Pam. He talked to Pam in the pool. He also helped her with one of her dives.

Pam, of course, didn't mind a bit. Don't get me wrong. Pam is a good friend of mine. But she definitely is a flirt. She always has a boyfriend, but never for very long. Her boyfriends are always jealous of the way she flirts with other guys.

Lisa came over and brought me some nachos. She also helped me get out of my lounge chair and inside to the bathroom.

"What am I going to do tomorrow, Lisa? How will I get around at school?" I asked desperately.

"I'll help you. And the other kids probably will, too," she said, opening the door for me. "Don't worry."

But I did worry. I worried about how I'd carry my notebooks to class, about what I'd wear, and about what everyone would say about my cast. But right now I worried about how Scott was watching Pam in her new black bikini.

Lisa said I was just imagining things. Scott did come back to talk with me before my dad came to get me. I had to leave at five. That was all I could talk my parents into. They thought I'd be too tired if I stayed any later.

I wasn't really prepared for all the attention I got at school the next day. *Everyone* wanted to know what had happened to my ankle. All the kids signed my cast, and most of my teachers did, too. I got a lot of comments like "Break a leg" and "Watch your step," but I didn't mind. It was fun to be the center of attention for a while. I even had a couple of guys offer to carry my books for me.

Our school has ramps everywhere, so I could get around okay. Sometimes I was late to class from walking so slowly. But my teachers didn't even mind if I was a little late to class. That was a surprise! Mr. Adams said I didn't need to make up the quiz I missed in math because I was the "walking wounded," as he put it. I started to think having a broken ankle might have some benefits after all.

I wasn't too far behind in my classes, since I had kept up with my work while I was at home. We were reviewing for our finals at the end of

27

the week. My biggest worry was what to wear to school. But on Monday Mom brought home two new dresses and a jeans skirt for me.

I wore one of my new dresses on Tuesday and got lots of compliments. Even Pam said she liked it when I thanked her for the pool party. She smiled and brushed back her blonde hair. Pam's hair, unlike mine, is always perfect.

"That Scott's really a sweet guy, you know," she said. "How long have you been going together?"

"A couple of months," I said. "Long enough to know we really like each other," as in, stay away, Perfect Pam, I thought. Find your own boyfriend. You're usually pretty good at it. I limped over to my desk and dropped one of my crutches as I sat down.

I obviously couldn't take gym class. So Mrs. Mac gave me a pass to study in the library. She talked to me in her office while the other girls were dressing for class.

I told her what Dr. Baum had said. And I told her I was sure I could get in shape for cheerleading in the fall.

"Practice starts August thirteenth, Charlie," she said. "You'd have to be ready by then," she said, looking doubtful.

"Just give me a chance," I pleaded. "If I'm not in shape you can tell me then. You know

28

how hard I've worked for this. I've taken all those ballet lessons and I've had hours of practice. I'm counting on being a cheerleader this fall. I just have to, Mrs. Mac."

"I know how important cheerleading is to you," she said. "But, as the poet said, 'the best laid plans of mice and men often go astray.' "

"What does that mean?" I asked. I didn't like the sound of it.

"Just because you plan something, and work for it and wish for it . . . that doesn't always make it come true," she said. "You're a good cheerleader with a good attitude, Charlie. But I have to do what's best for the whole squad."

Mrs. Mac gave my shoulder a squeeze. "I'll talk to you and your parents in August. Then we'll decide. I'm just sorry you won't be with us at cheerleading camp," she said.

You're sorry, I thought. Not half as sorry as I am! What a bummer!

Five

I had to study hard that week for my finals. Scott only called once because he was busy studying, too.

On Wednesday and Thursday we had finals all day. Friday was just a half day of school. We picked up our yearbooks and got our final grades in each class. I got four B's, an A in math and a C in history. I knew Dad wouldn't like the C.

Mom came in to school to pick me up so she could carry all my things home for me. She had to leave her volunteer job to come get me. Mom volunteers three days a week at our community center. It's called the Hub. She's the publicity director there, planning classes and programs. She's trying to turn it into a paying job.

I had the whole afternoon ahead of me after Mom went back to the Hub. Lisa had gone shopping with Pam for new clothes for camp. I called Scott, but he was out on his motorbike.

I decided to sit outside and work on my tan.

I put the strap of my tape player over my shoulder and put some favorite tapes in the pocket of my shorts. I dumped my suntan oil and some magazines in my book bag and toted everything out to the deck. It was not easy to move things around when you had to walk with crutches. Plus, my leg was really starting to itch inside my cast.

I wanted some iced tea. But I didn't want to get up and go all the way into the kitchen again.

I need a maid, I thought. Anyone with a broken ankle should have her own maid, maybe a robot.

"Yes * Miss * Charlie. * Here * is * your * iced * tea. * May * I * offer * you * some * cookies? * Let * me * fan * your * face. * This * is * a * recording." * Beep. * Beep.*

Maybe I could get a robot that looked like Dr. Baum . . . and made house calls. I fell asleep dreaming about an entire cheerleading squad of robots. And each one had a cast on her right leg.

Mom took me to the library Saturday morning to get some books to keep me busy. I like to read, but not all day for a whole summer. There didn't seem to be much else to do.

It was such a let-down to be home all by

myself. I missed all the attention I'd been getting at school. What good was a cast on your leg if you had to stay home all alone? I wondered. I felt trapped in the cast, too.

Dad tried to cheer me up when he got home from golf. "I know this has been a big disappointment for you, Honey. But I'm planning something that will help you pass the time."

"What, Dad?" I couldn't guess what he meant. "A new T.V. video game, maybe?" I asked.

"No, not quite," he said. "It's more educational than that." Dad was being very mysterious. "You'll know in about a week."

My dad is very big on anything educational. He's an educational consultant and travels all over the country giving programs for different businesses. He tells people how to be more creative and how to get more work done faster. Dad has an office here in town, but he travels almost every week.

"I'm going to try to be home more this summer, too," Dad said. "I'm thinking of writing a book about my business programs." Mom called us to dinner just then.

Scott came over for a while later that night. We sat outside on the deck and Scott told me about his new job.

"Pam was at the pool with Lisa today," he

said. "Pam's back one-and-a-half pike is coming right along."

"What's a back one-and-a-half pike?" I asked. I really didn't want to talk about Pam.

"You know, that's the dive I've been helping her with . . . a backward flip with one-and-a-half rotations," he said, demonstrating the dive with his hands. "And it's in the pike position. Know what that is?"

"Nope," I mumbled. My leg was itching and I felt hot. Who wanted to hear about some stupid dive? I wondered. I couldn't even do a plain dive off the diving board. The spring of the board scared me.

Mom came out on the deck and asked if we wanted some ice cream. Scott left soon after that. I guess he knew I was tired.

I talked to Lisa on Sunday. She was going to a family reunion that day. I guess Scott must have gone, too. He didn't call me. And there was no answer when I called his house.

On Monday we went to see Dr. Baum for a new cast. He was even more handsome than when I saw him in the hospital. I wondered if he was married. He didn't wear a wedding ring.

"Okay, here we go with the saw again," he said. "Anyone for leg of cheerleader?" he asked, laughing. Dr. Baum neatly sliced through the autographs on my old cast.

My leg looked terrible to me with the cast off. Of course it had hair growing all over it. And it didn't smell very good either.

Dr. Baum was peeling off the little pieces of tape over my incision. "Let's take off these butterfly bandages," he said. "Good. Your incision is healing nicely," he finally commented.

He had one of his nurses X-ray my leg again. This time he showed us the X rays. "See, right here the bone is healing," he said. "And here is the wire and the screw we put in to hold the bone together until it's well-healed. We'll take those out in six months or so, maybe on your Christmas vacation."

Oh, great, I thought. Then my Christmas vacation could be ruined just like my summer vacation.

Dr. Baum was spreading more white goo on my leg. In a few minutes my leg was covered again by a new white cast.

"Now, here's a cast boot to put over your foot," Dr. Baum said. He put a plastic sort of shoe on my foot and laced it up. "It has what we call a rocker bottom. You can start putting some weight on your ankle now. But keep using your crutches, too. Any questions?" he asked.

"No, no questions," I said. Except what am I going to do all summer? I wondered.

My first full week at home dragged by. Lisa and Pam had cheerleading practice every afternoon to get ready for camp. Mom was busy with summer classes at the Hub. She took an exercise class almost every day, too, so she was gone a lot. Dad was in New York.

I read my library books, listened to tapes, watched T.V. I got so tired of sitting around all the time! I missed jogging and ballet classes, and going to the mall with my friends.

Scott was busy with his job at the pool and mowing lawns in his neighborhood. He didn't call me every night any more. He must have been out riding his motorbike a lot . . . by himself, I hoped.

Lisa called on Friday to say good-bye. The cheerleading squad was leaving for camp early on Saturday.

"I have everything packed already," Lisa said, bubbling with excitement. "We have three different outfits to wear at camp. We have white shorts with school T-shirts for hot weather, jeans and school sweatshirts for cool weather, and our cheerleading skirts and vests for competition. It's too hot to wear our regular sweaters, you know."

She went on and on about the clothes she was taking. The squad had planned all their outfits after I broke my ankle.

"Did you practice my cheer this week?" I

asked. I tried to get Lisa off the subject of her camp wardrobe.

"Oh, Charlie! You should see it!" she bubbled.

"See it? I wrote it, remember?" I reminded her.

"We're calling it Tower of Power. We're using your words, but we made up new actions. Terri, Jill, and Karen kneel on the floor. Pam and I stand on their backs and then leap off. So it's like an exploding tower of power, you know?"

"Sounds good," I muttered. Why did they have to change the actions? It was *my* cheer. It helped me make the squad.

Lisa finally stopped talking about herself. "How are things going with Scott?" she asked.

"Okay, I guess. He's pretty busy with his job," I said. I didn't feel like telling her I hadn't seen him in almost a week.

"Yeah, Pam and I saw him at the pool yesterday," Lisa said. "We went swimming after practice. He helped Pam with her dive again during his break."

"What is it with her?" I asked. I tried to keep the anger out of my voice. "I hope she knows Scott is *my* boyfriend."

"She did say she thinks he's really cute. Want me to say something to her about it?" she asked. Lisa's voice was concerned.

"No, better not," I said. I didn't want Scott to think I was jealous, even if I was.

"Have to run," Lisa said. "We'll think of you every day."

"Have a good time at camp," I said.

"Oh, I wish you could come, Charlie. Write to me!" she added.

Sure, I thought as I hung up the phone. I won't have anything else to do.

Six

MY parents tried to cheer me up on Saturday. Mom took me to my favorite store in the mall that morning. I got a new casual dress that looked okay with my cast, and some pink shorts. We bought Dad a new bathrobe for Father's Day.

They took me out for pizza for dinner. I called Scott to ask him to go with us. But he was going to see a new horror movie with his friend Mark.

There's nothing like going out with your parents on a Saturday night, I thought. Everyone at the pizza place stared at my cast and crutches. They probably wondered why I was such a klutz.

By the time we got home I was really depressed. Mom and Dad tried hard. But there wasn't that much they could do. All I wanted was to be eighty miles away at camp with the rest of the cheerleading squad.

Dad gave me a big hug before I went to my

room. "Wait till tomorrow, Honey. I think you need a big surprise to help cheer you up," he said.

"A new leg, Dad. That's what I need. Just sign me up for a transplant and I'll be happy," I said.

I went to bed early and read my horoscope for June in one of my magazines.

"June is a dangerous month for you. A major break will occur in your personal life." Bingo! Maybe there was something to horoscopes. I kept reading. "A friend will prove untrue." Wonder what that meant. I hoped that part didn't apply to me.

The next morning Mom and I made Dad's favorite breakfast—bacon and eggs and cinnamon rolls. Dad wore his new plaid robe.

Later we drove to Grand Ledge to have dinner with Dad's parents. Grandma and Grandpa hadn't seen my cast yet. They made a huge fuss over me. They told me all about how my Aunt Laurie had broken her leg in junior high. She broke hers by jumping off their back porch! At least I broke mine in an accident and not just by being clumsy.

We got home about five. Dad told me to wait in my bedroom while he got the surprise ready. He and Mom both seemed pretty excited. I decided it must be a T.V. for my room. Then I wouldn't have to get up to use the one in the family room.

"You can come out now, Charlie. It's ready!" Dad sounded excited and proud.

I got my crutches and walked out to the family room. On the desk was a computer.

"Wow, Dad! You got yourself a computer. Happy Father's Day!" I said, giving him a hug.

"But it's not just for me," he said. "It's mostly for you, to have fun with this summer."

Now, I have never touched a computer. I wasn't really planning to, either. You're talking to the mechanical midget here, I wanted to tell Dad. I'm the girl who called you at your office for instructions on using a hand-operated can opener. The electric one was broken.

"But Dad . . . I don't know anything about computers," I said. And I don't care to, either, I thought. Computers are for those weird, smart guys. You know, the ones with six pens in their shirt pockets and calculators on their belts.

"No problem," Dad said. He really was proud of himself. "Tomorrow you and I go for training on our new Apple IIc. That's the name of this baby." He patted the top of the computer.

"See, we have all these books and computer magazines, too. It's a whole new world, Charlie. You'll love it," he said excitedly.

Or else, I thought. "Well, you can get games

for computers, right, Dad?" I asked. I tried to think of something positive to say.

"Sure! And you can do your papers for school, charts, graphs, you name it! And I'm going to use it to write my book."

My mom gave me a knowing smile behind my dad's head. Sometimes we have to humor my dad when he has a new idea. After all, being creative is part of his business.

"Oh, by the way," Dad said, "do you know a boy named David Evans? I think he's a year ahead of you in school."

"I know who he is," I answered. "Why?"

"Well, his dad's a client of mine. He owns his own construction firm. David is a real computer whiz, from what his dad tells me."

"I know David Evans," Mom said. "He teaches a computer class for kids at the Hub. He's a very nice young man."

Dad was beaming. "David's coming over later this week to give us some pointers," he said.

As I recall, David Evans is about six feet tall and has thick glasses. He warms the bench during every basketball game. Oh, well, I could humor Dad, I thought. He was trying hard to be nice.

"It'll be fun, Dad. Thanks a lot," I said. I gave him another hug.

"I'll get things all set up tonight," Dad said.

"Then we'll be ready to go tomorrow morning. Ten o'clock, we report to Computer City for training!"

Scott called just then, so I was excused from the computer pep talk. My dad could teach the cheerleading squad a thing or two.

I told Scott all about Dad's new computer. "And I have to learn how to use it," I said. "Dad has his heart set on it."

Scott just laughed. He has the nicest laugh. I could just imagine how he looked talking on the phone. He has straight blond hair and bright blue eyes. I loved his eyes from the minute I saw them.

"You'll like having a computer," he said. "They're fun. You remember, I told you I took Introduction to Computers in ninth grade. Maybe you should take that next year."

"Oh, that's all I need. I have enough trouble keeping up my grades as it is," I said. I shifted my weight, trying to get my cast in a more comfortable position. "When can you come over, Scott?" I asked.

"Not sure," he said. "I'm pretty busy this week. I'm working full time at the pool now and still mowing lawns, too. And I'm trying to swim at the pool before or after work."

And you're helping cute girls with their dives, I'll bet, I wanted to say. There was an awkward pause when no one said anything.

"I'm riding my motorbike a lot, too," Scott added. "Mark got his last week. So we go out together and ride a lot."

And a girl with a cast on her leg just doesn't fit in, I thought.

"Well, come over sometime soon." I tried to sound cheerful. "I miss you," I said sweetly.

"Okay. See you," he said.

"Bye, Scott." Something was missing, I thought as I hung up the phone. Scott just wasn't as interested in me as he used to be. I just wish I didn't have this stupid cast, I thought. Then I could be the one out riding with Scott, instead of Mark.

Seven

THE next morning Dad got me up early. He made breakfast for us since Mom was already at work. Dad was really excited about his computer. He reminded me of a little boy with a new toy. He was the way Scott was when he first got his motorbike. That was all Scott could talk about for days.

Dad talked about computers all through breakfast. He already had a computer at work. But he hadn't used it much. Mainly his secretary used it for the reports he sent to his clients.

"The best thing," Dad was saying, "is that our computer at the office is an Apple II. That means it's compatible with the one we have at home."

"What's compatible?" I asked.

"Well, they can use the same programs," he said. "I could bring work home from the office and do it here on this computer. Or you could even do some work here for me that I could use at the office. How does that sound to you?"

"Work?" I pretended to be horrified. "This is my summer *vacation,* you know."

"I'd pay you, silly," Dad said with a smile. He helped me up and handed me my crutches. "It's just something to think about."

We arrived at Computer City a few minutes early. We were greeted by a tall woman in a tan suit.

"Good morning, Mr. Hunter. Good to see you again," she said, shaking my Dad's hand. "And you must be Charlie. It's nice to meet you. I'm your sales representative, Joyce Nelson." She shook my hand, too. She didn't even mention my broken ankle.

Joyce had us sit down in front of an Apple IIc computer just like the one at home. She explained the computer's display screen, keyboard and the printer. "That's called hardware," she said.

Next Joyce held out a thin square of plastic with a hole in the center. "Now this is an example of software. The programs that tell the computer what to do are called software," she said. She handed me the plastic square. "This is called a floppy disk, or disk for short. Hold it by the edges, Charlie. Be careful not to touch the inside layer of plastic. That's what the computer uses to read and write information."

Then Joyce slid the floppy disk into the side of the computer. "That's how you load a disk. This model is great because it has a built-in disk drive. Simple, right? Now the program I just loaded is for beginners. It's called a tutorial because it teaches you about the computer. You give it a try and I'll be back in a few minutes," she said

Dad and I read the instructions on the screen. It showed us a cute little man and house. Then it gave us easy instructions to follow. We learned how to erase mistakes, and what a cursor is. That's a little blinking line that moves around the screen to give your location.

Whenever we did the right thing, the computer wrote out something like "Great!" or "Good job!" If we made a mistake, it told us that and said, "Try again." We learned that that meant the computer was user-friendly. Whoever thought of a computer as friendly? We read that programs that aren't user-friendly say "NO! WRONG!" Dad and I laughed at the little jokes that appeared on the screen.

"This is more fun than I thought it would be, Dad," I told him. He seemed pleased. Next the computer asked me to type in my first name. I haven't taken typing in school yet. So I had to search for each letter.

"Very good, Charlie," the screen said. Next it showed CHARLIE'S MENU. We read that a menu is a list of things the program can do. You pick an item from the menu and go to that choice. Dad and I took turns picking from the menu. Each menu item taught us something new.

Joyce came back to our worktable. "How's it going?" she asked.

"Great!" I said. "This is really fun. Can we buy one of these tutorials?" I wanted to practice it all again at home.

"Oh, that tutorial comes with your computer," Joyce said. "You should already have that disk at home. Five disks and three manuals come with your Apple model." Joyce set some small packages on our table. "I've selected some additional software for you as you asked, Mr. Hunter."

Joyce showed us our new word processing program. "That's your most important piece of software," she said. "It makes your computer work like a very smart typewriter. You use it to create a new document or edit an old one. And you use it to print out hard copy. That's a copy of your work on regular paper."

Joyce demonstrated how the printer worked. "This long paper in your printer is called fan-fold," she said. We watched as the printer buzzed back and forth. It seemed to print a whole line of type at a time!

"See, each sheet of paper has tiny holes at the end of each page. You just tear them apart," Joyce added. She showed us how to do it.

"Now, I think Charlie would like this learn-to-type program," Joyce said, smiling at me. "This is the top-selling one in the country. And it's a fun way to learn typing."

I did want to learn how to type. It took too long to search for each letter or number on the keyboard.

"This is one of our most popular educational games," Joyce said, showing us a brightly colored package. "It's a fantasy-adventure game that teaches logic. You also have some other games on the disks that come with the computer."

"Fine," Dad said as he got up. "Charlie, why don't you see if there are any books on computers you'd like to have."

I went over to one wall where there was a huge display of books on computers. I picked out a book on Apple computers for kids. Dad paid for the book and we said good-bye to Joyce.

"Come in again if you want more help," she said. "And don't forget to read your manuals! Have fun with your Apple, Charlie!"

In the next few days, Dad and I spent a lot

of time at the computer. We practiced the tutorial until we had all the basics down. I tried to memorize the keyboard so I could type faster.

The learn-to-type program was really fun. It flashed words and numbers on the screen. Then you had to type them back quickly or have alien invaders blast your spaceship. I decided that it was more fun to learn to type this way instead of in school.

Scott didn't call on Monday or Tuesday. Dad and I played the adventure game on the computer. We learned how to play the other games that came on the extra disks. I practiced my typing program during the day. I wanted to be able to type a letter to Lisa at camp.

On Wednesday Dad called me from his office. "Charlie, that guy I was telling you about is coming over tonight. You remember, David Evans? Is that okay with you?" he asked.

I didn't think I'd like this David too much. He wasn't that popular at school. But I didn't mind if he helped us with the computer.

"Sure, Dad. I don't have any plans," I said.

David Evans arrived about seven. He wasn't wearing his glasses anymore. Maybe he had contacts now. He seemed very polite and made a good impression on my parents. David had lots of experience with Apple computers.

"Next year I'm taking a computer programming class in high school," he told Dad. "I'm really looking forward to it."

He showed us how to save our work on the computer by copying it onto a blank disk. We showed him our adventure game and he tried it out.

"I've got lots of games at home," he said. "Maybe I could bring them over so you could see which ones you like."

Actually David was pretty nice, I decided. He didn't have the greatest looks in the world. But without his glasses he didn't look bad. In fact, he was kind of cute.

Dad went out to the kitchen to get us some lemonade. David asked, "What do you do Tuesday afternoons?"

Sit around and stare at my cast, I thought. What do you think? "Not much," I said. "Why?" No point in being sarcastic.

"That's when I teach my class on computers at the Hub. I thought you might like to come," he suggested.

"Well . . . maybe," I said. "I'll have to see if Mom could take me."

David stood closer to the computer to load a different disk. He was leaning over next to me, and he put his hand on my shoulder. I looked up into his face. He really did have a nice smile. Even his eyes sparkled a little.

"Charlie," Dad said from the doorway. "Scott's here."

Eight

Dear Lisa,

I'll bet you're surprised to get a
letter typed by *me*. And this wasn't
typed on an old-fashioned typewriter either! Dad bought us an
Apple computer so I can keep busy
this summer. I'm having fun with it
so far. I can already type 18 words
a minute. I'll show you how to use
the computer as soon as you get
back.

You won't *believe* what happened
Wednesday night. I think Scott is
really mad at me. We had this guy
over helping us with the computer—
David Evans. You know who he is, I
think. He was on the basketball team
last year.

Anyway, David was pretty close to me, helping me with the computer, and Scott walked in. He looked furious! I hardly even know David (yet). So I don't know what Scott was so mad about.

David left right after Scott got here. And then Scott left after only half an hour. He said he had to be home by ten. But I think he was just mad. He didn't even kiss me good-bye.

He hasn't been seeing me that much lately. I think it's because of my cast. I wish I could ride on his motorbike this summer!

How is cheerleading camp so far? Are you learning lots of new cheers? Send me a postcard.

Miss you,

Charlie

I checked my letter for mistakes and corrected them. Then I printed out a copy of my letter. It looked very professional, especially for someone who couldn't type at all a week ago.

My days were getting into a pattern. In the mornings I used the computer. I practiced my typing a lot and played the other games. I was really having fun with one program that made the computer beep out little songs. I was trying to get it to play our school song.

After lunch I watched a couple of soap operas, read my library books and took a nap. After dinner Dad and I used the computer together. And every night I hoped Scott would call.

I don't like to call guys that much. Mom doesn't approve of it, anyway. By Friday night I couldn't stand waiting around any more. I called, but Scott wasn't home. His mom said she'd have him call me, but he never did.

On Sunday night I called him again.

"Hi, Scott. This is Charlie," I said trying to sound casual.

"Hi."

"How are things going?" I asked.

"Fine." Scott still sounded mad.

"Well, what have you been doing?" I asked. Why was he being so difficult?

"Working," he snapped. I already knew that.

"What's the problem here, Scott? Are you still mad about the other night?" I asked. I was starting to get a little mad myself.

"Oh, no, I'm not mad. I like coming over to see you and seeing some other guy falling all over you," he said.

"Scott, wait. I told you David is a friend of

Dad's. He didn't come over to see me," I reminded him.

Silence.

"And even if he had . . ." I didn't know what to say next. "Well, you hardly ever call or come over any more! What do you expect, anyway?" I asked practically shouting. *Click*. I couldn't believe it. He hung up on me.

At first I was really mad. But then I calmed down and was only hurt. Later I started thinking about how much Scott meant to me, how sweet and understanding he used to be, and how much I loved those blue eyes. By the time I tried to go to sleep I was crying.

The next day Mom took me to the doctor to have my ankle X-rayed. I saw Dr. Baum again. I hoped he wouldn't notice my red eyes.

"You're coming along just fine, Charlie," Dr. Baum said.

My leg, maybe, I thought, but not my love life.

"You can put more weight on your ankle now," he said. "Start phasing out the crutches, but do it gradually."

I would sure be glad to be rid of those stupid crutches. They made everyone stare at me. Maybe, when I could get along without crutches, I could start going out more. But then, with whom would I go anywhere? I wondered.

That week was really boring, and hot. The heat wave we were having was making my leg itch in that cast. I tried to scratch it with a straightened-out coat hanger. But that didn't help much.

The only interesting thing I did all week was go to David's computer class. There were seven kids in the class. Most of them were in elementary school. David used the Hub's Apple computer to teach the class. He was pretty good at explaining things to the kids.

After the class was over, he sat with me waiting for my dad to pick me up. The Hub is right across from the community pool. I looked for Scott's motorbike outside. But it wasn't there.

"Why don't you come to class every week, Charlie?" David asked. "You'll be able to help me with the younger kids."

"Okay. I'll try. Oh, there's Dad. Gotta run," I said. Well, gotta limp along, I should have said. It was a lot easier to get around now that I could put more weight on my ankle. I tried not to rush giving up my crutches. But it was so nice to *walk* again. I didn't need my crutches at all by the end of the week.

Lisa got home from camp on Saturday. We had lots to talk about, so she came over to spend the night. She showed me all the new cheers they learned. She told me all about the other squads, and all the funny things that happened. It was all the fun that I missed.

"You really missed something during one practice," Lisa said, laughing. "Pam fell during our school song routine. *Everyone* saw her." Lisa demonstrated how Pam had fallen. I could certainly see how it must have been funny.

Lisa said she was planning a big party at her house for the Fourth of July. "Don't worry, Charlie," she said. "I'll call Scott and get him to come to the party. Then you two can, you know, work things out."

That night we were talking before we went to sleep. It was late and I knew Lisa was tired. But I had to ask her.

"Lisa, you do think Scott really likes me, don't you?" I asked. "Maybe he'll get over being mad at me."

"He told me he really liked you a lot," she said. "At least he did before I went to camp."

I thought Lisa had fallen asleep. Then suddenly she asked, "Charlie, you awake?"

"Mmmm," I mumbled sleepily.

"There's something else I have to tell you." The dark silence of my room pressed in on me. Lisa went on. "I didn't want to tell you this. But I think you should know," she said.

I was wide awake.

"Scott wrote to Pam while we were at camp.

I saw his handwriting and return address on the envelope."

* * * * * *

I talked to Lisa again on Tuesday morning.

"Charlie, I hate to tell you this," she said. "But Scott said he can't come to my party. He said he's going away for the day. But he wouldn't say where."

"Well, maybe he's going motorbike riding with his friend Mark," I said. "He probably just doesn't want to see me."

"But there's something else," Lisa said. "Pam can't come either. She's going to the beach with her family for the day."

"You don't think . . ." That little sneak, I thought.

"Yeah, I do, Charlie. I'm really sorry," Lisa said.

That afternoon Mom took me to David's computer class again. I was looking forward to helping the younger kids. David seemed glad to have me there.

After class David and I walked out together again. We sat down and talked about his new computer chess program. I heard a familiar putt, putt, vroom! across the parking lot. Scott backed his motorbike up and then drove right past us. He looked right at me and looked away again, like he didn't even know me! But the girl on the back smiled at us. She took one hand away from Scott's waist and waved.

It was Pam.

Nine

LISA'S Fourth of July party would have been fun if only Scott had been there with me. It had been a long time since I'd been to a party without him. And I couldn't forget I'd met Scott at Lisa's last party.

Lisa's dad cooked hamburgers on the grill for all of us. Then everyone played volleyball till dark. I kept score. About nine o'clock Lisa brought out big slices of watermelon and boxes of sparklers. A couple of the guys shot off some firecrackers until Lisa's dad made them stop.

We could see the city's fireworks display from the backyard. Everyone said "ooh" at each burst of color and then we all laughed just like we do every year. But this year the fireworks should have been special. I kept thinking how Scott's arm should have been around my shoulders as we watched the fireworks. I was also wondering if he was kissing Pam at that very moment.

I called Dad to pick me up as soon as the fireworks were over. Lisa was planning ice cream sundaes. But I just wanted to go home and go to sleep. I wasn't in a partying mood.

Dad tried to talk to me about Scott on the way home. But how can you talk about your boyfriend to your father? I wondered.

We stopped at a red light. "It hasn't been the best summer for you, has it, Charlie?" Dad asked.

"You could say that," I answered.

"Could be worse, you know." Dad always says that.

"Oh, come on, Dad. I missed cheerleading camp. I have a cast on my leg for most of the summer. And my boyfriend just broke up with me! How could that get worse?" I asked.

"Cheer up, Charlie. Your leg is healing fine now. Your accident could have been worse. You could be in the hospital in traction or in a cast up to your hip," Dad said. He reached over and patted me on the shoulder. "Scott's not the only fish in the sea, you know."

But he's the one I want, I thought. That night, before bed, I wrote Scott a letter trying to make things better between us. I told him how much I missed him, that I was sorry about our fight, and that I still wanted him as my boyfriend. We had never said we loved each other. But I signed, "Love always, Charlie."

I was putting my letter in the mailbox the next morning when David called. I hobbled to the phone.

"I was wondering if I could bring my computer programs over tomorrow night to show you and your dad?" he asked. He was a very polite guy, just like Mom said.

"Well, I'll have to check with Dad," I said. "It would be okay with me."

We talked for a few minutes about his computer class. David said he'd call later to check about Friday night.

I wasn't really interested in David as a boyfriend. It was just nice to have plans with a guy on the weekend anyway.

Dad seemed glad to hear David was coming over. "I like that young man," he said. "He seems very responsible."

On Friday afternoon Dad offered me a job. He said he'd pay me two dollars an hour to do some computer work for him. He needed his mailing lists from the office put on computer disk.

"You can go at your own pace, Charlie," Dad said, "as long as you have it done before school starts." He showed me his filing system. There were hundreds of names and addresses on little white cards. It didn't look like the most interesting project. But I was glad to have a paying job.

"I thought David could get you started on this," Dad said, "just to get things headed in the right direction." Okay, Dad, I thought. I was beginning to get the idea—about which direction Dad would like things to go with David.

That night David brought all kinds of software over to our house to show us. We tried out his new chess program. Dad really liked that because chess is one of his favorite games. He worked at trying to beat the computer at chess. David started helping me with my mailing list project.

We ordered a pizza about ten o'clock, and Mom and Dad went to pick it up. David and I sat and talked about computers, school and summer vacation. By the time he left that night I had decided he was a really nice person. I was pretty sure the feeling was mutual.

Lisa went camping with her family the next week, so I was pretty lonely. I spent several hours a day working on Dad's mailing list. I sat out in the sun reading David's computer magazines. Mom took me in for more X rays. And David called twice to see how I was getting along with the computer.

On Saturday night David came over to show Dad some more computer stuff. He was trying to talk Dad into buying more hardware. "Add-ons," he called them. They were talking about video displays, color monitors, disk drives, all kinds of technical stuff.

Dad started playing David's chess game again. So David came over and sat down with Mom and me to watch a movie Mom had rented. It was nice having David there, except I wasn't sure if he'd come to see Dad . . . or me.

Ten

ON Monday morning I was up and dressed early. After seven weeks I was finally going to get rid of that stupid cast. I couldn't wait to come home and take my first shower in seven weeks! I was sick of baths and having to hang that heavy cast out the side of the bathtub.

My doctor's appointment wasn't till eleven so I spent extra time on my hair and makeup. Then I worked on my address project until Mom came home to get me.

"Excited to get that cast off, Charlie?" she asked with a smile.

"Are you kidding?" I said, grabbing my purse. "Let's go. I can't wait."

We waited about half an hour to see the doctor. Finally we got to see Dr. Baum.

"Well, this is the big day," he said. He was even more handsome when he smiled. "Are you ready to have two working ankles again?"

"Ready when you are," I answered.

Dr. Baum turned on his electric saw, and my

cast was off in a few seconds.

My leg looked awful. It was white, hairy, skinny and smelly. I burst into tears in front of Dr. Baum, again.

"Hey, Charlie, it's okay," he said. He even put his arm around me. "Everyone's leg looks like that after being in a cast for weeks."

"But . . . but I thought it would be healed," I mumbled. Why did I always sound so dumb around him? I wondered.

"You are healed, Charlie." Dr. Baum helped me up. "Everything looks good. You can resume normal activities, but nothing athletic. Walking is okay, but no running."

"What about cheerleading?" I asked. Practice started in only a month.

"Come back in, oh, say four weeks and we'll check it out," Dr. Baum said. He wrote on my records. "You can try some heel-lifts standing on stair steps to get back in shape." He showed me the exercise. "Just don't overdo. See you in a month."

It felt so strange to walk again without a cast. My leg felt like it had just been let out of prison.

I went straight into the bathroom as soon as we got home. My leg felt a little better once I was done with my shower. But my calf was so thin and white. My left leg was pretty tan from sitting out in the sun so much. But my right leg from the knee down was *white*. Wearing shorts was out. I'd have to stick to pants.

Lisa called the next day to ask me to go to the pool, of all places.

"I can't go there, Lisa!" I wailed. "I'll see Scott. He'll see my white leg!"

"Oh, come on, Charlie," Lisa said. "Don't be such a chicken. So what if you do see him? It's a public pool, you know. He'll be busy working, anyway."

Lisa's mom took us to the pool that afternoon. I put some tanning gel makeup on my leg so it didn't look so white. My calf was so skinny, though. I decided I'd have to get back in shape right away.

There weren't many people at the pool when we got there. Scott wasn't there, either. We did see two of the other cheerleaders, Terri and Karen. So we all sat together and talked about cheerleading camp. After a while I decided to try swimming just a little. The cool water felt wonderful. I couldn't believe I hadn't been swimming all summer. What a waste.

I swam a few widths, slowly, with an easy sidestroke. When I went back to the other girls, I could tell by their faces something was up.

"Scott's here," Terri whispered.

I looked over and saw Scott at the wading

pool. He was staring right at me. I smiled and waved to him. I didn't know what else to do. He gave a little wave back and turned and walked back into the locker rooms. I didn't see him again.

I left the pool and dressed in my pink striped jeans and pink shirt. Then I went over to David's computer class at the Hub.

"Wow, Charlie!" David said. "You got your cast off. You look great."

"I feel great, too," I told him.

David's class that day was fun. He showed us a computer mouse. A computer mouse is a little pointing tool you hold in your hand. It's connected to the computer by a long electrical cord. That's the mouse's "tail," I guess. The little kids loved using the mouse because they didn't have to type so much. They used the mouse and a graphics program to draw circles, squares and flowers.

After the class, Mom and Dad took me out to dinner. We all celebrated with a "No More Cast" dinner at Captain Crablegs restaurant.

I went up to my room early that night. I felt so much better, so full of energy. I decided to try some exercises, just to get back in shape, like a few toe-touches, leg-lifts, sit-ups. What could it hurt? I wondered. I knew my ankle was healed.

The next day Lisa asked me to go to the

mall with her. I had really missed shopping with Lisa.

We visited all our favorite stores from one end of the mall to the other. We checked out all the summer sales. We even tried on some of the new fall clothes.

My ankle was getting sore by the time we got home. I used the computer till dinner time. After dinner I helped Mom clean up the kitchen.

"I'm going out for a walk, okay?" I asked.

"Sure, Honey. The doctor said you could," Mom answered.

I walked for a couple of blocks. Then I started jogging. It was wonderful to be running again! I ran for about two more blocks. Then I turned around and jogged most of the way home. My ankle hardly hurt at all.

I exercised in my room again that night before bedtime. I was determined to get back in shape, even if it hurt a little. After all, I thought, no pain, no gain. But I was wrong.

"Mom! Come here!" I yelled the next morning. My digital clock said 5:43. My ankle was swollen, and it hurt. It really hurt.

"Oh, Charlie, no," Mom said. "You must have overdone it yesterday."

Dad got me some pain medication. We waited a while but the pain got worse. Mom talked to Dr. Baum at about seven.

"Let me help you get dressed," Mom said when she came back. By then I was crying. "We're meeting the doctor in the emergency room right away. He said you may have re-established the fracture line."

"What does that mean?" I sobbed.

Dad put his arms around me. "You may have rebroken your ankle, Honey."

Eleven

"CHARLIE, I heard you broke your ankle again!" Lisa said. She telephoned early on Friday morning. "Is it true?"

"No, it's not broken again," I answered. "I just did too much too soon. That's the good news."

"What's the bad news?" Lisa asked.

"I'm in a cast again. And it doesn't come off till four weeks from now," I said.

"Four weeks! But cheerleading practice starts before then," Lisa said. She sounded like she didn't believe my news.

"I know. Dr. Baum said I couldn't cheer this fall," I said. I had to try hard to keep from crying.

"Oh, Charlie, that's awful," Lisa said. "I'm really sorry."

Lisa tried to make me feel better. But nothing she said helped at all. I was off the squad. And I'd probably never get back on. That's all there was to it.

"I'd better go, Lisa," I said.

"Wait . . . we're all going to the county fair this weekend. Do you think you could come?" she asked.

"Now, how could I walk around a fair?" I asked. I didn't mean to sound so crabby. "I have to keep my ankle up for a whole week, anyway. And this time I'm doing what they tell me."

"Well, okay," Lisa said. She sounded a little hurt. "I'll call you and tell you how the fair was."

For the next week I sat at my computer all day, every day. I worked on Dad's mailing list until I finished putting it on disk. He couldn't believe I was finished so quickly.

"You did a great job, Charlie," Dad said. "This is really going to help me improve business." He looked over the final printed copy of his mailing list. "I'll bring home your paycheck tomorrow."

After I finished the mailing list, I didn't have any other computer project to work on. I practiced the typing program. I played all the computer games we had. Dad even bought me a new one. But I could only do that for so long.

I kept thinking about cheerleading. I couldn't get it out of my mind. Our cheers . . . they kept running through my mind over and over, especially one called Success.

S-U-C-C-E-S-S!
That's the way
To spell success!

Being a cheerleader meant success at Evergreen Junior High. I had fought hard for that success.

Go! Fight! Win!
Hey, hey, hey,
GO!
FIGHT!
WIN!

I had found out that fighters don't always win. Sometimes they lose.

That night I started putting some cheers on the computer. I didn't really have anything else to do. I thought maybe Lisa would like a copy of all the cheers. I wanted to remember them, too.

The next day Mom took me in for X rays. Dr. Moyer said I could start walking on crutches again. He also said I still had to have my cast on for three more weeks.

I called Mrs. Mac that night to tell her I had to quit cheerleading. It was one of the hardest things I ever had to do.

"I'm really sorry, Mrs. Mac. I hate to let the squad down," I said.

"We'll certainly miss you, Charlie," Mrs.

Mac said in her crisp way. "The squad just won't be the same without you."

"I guess you'll get a replacement for me?" I asked.

"I'll have to move someone up from the junior varsity squad, I think," Mrs. Mac said. "Stop by the school one day during practice, if you like. We'd all be glad to see you."

I didn't say if I would come or not. It would be pretty hard to watch someone else cheering in my place.

On Friday I thought up cheers and typed them into the computer. Sometimes I added notes about the motions for the cheers. If it was one of our original cheers, I put down who wrote it. When I entered my Tower of Power cheer, I typed in "by Charlie Hunter." Might as well give myself some credit, I thought.

By late Friday afternoon I had almost all the cheers on the computer. I saved the file on disk and turned off the computer. Just as I was unloading the disk, I heard the phone ring. I didn't have time to put the disk away. It always took me so long to get to the phone on crutches. So I took the disk with me and set it down carefully next to the phone. I didn't want anything to happen to it.

Mom was on the phone. She wanted me to put some frozen dinners in the oven. After I got done talking to her I got some iced tea.

The phone rang again and this time it was David.

"We missed you in class last week," he said. "Sorry to hear about your ankle."

I told him how it had happened.

"You sound like you need a break. Uh, no pun intended there," he laughed. "Anyway, would you like to go to the movies with me tomorrow night?"

I didn't know what to say. I wanted David for a friend. But I wasn't sure about anything more than that. And what if someone saw us at the movies and told Scott? I wondered.

"I—I'm still on crutches, you know," I said. "It's really too hard for me to get around yet. Maybe you could just come over here again. I'd like you to see my new project— Cheerleading by Computer, you could call it."

"Okay," David said. He sounded agreeable enough. "See you about seven-thirty?"

I said good-bye and took my disk back to the computer. I had just thought of another cheer to enter.

I loaded the disk and typed in the name of the file: CHEERS. The screen read, FILE NOT FOUND. But I knew that couldn't be right. I had just been working on the cheers a few minutes ago. I checked again. The disk was blank. Somehow my cheers had all been erased.

I looked up David's telephone number and called him back.

"Did you leave the disk in the computer the whole time?" he asked.

"No, I had it right here with me in the kitchen," I said. "I put it right beside the phone and—"

"Did the phone ring?" he interrupted.

"Well, yes. Mom was calling. And then you called," I said.

"That explains it then," David said. "See, your floppy disk is a magnetic recording device. The bell in the telephone is an electromagnet. When the phone rings it sets up an electromagnetic field. That's what erased your disk."

"You mean now I have to enter all those cheers all over again?" I asked, furious. "I had about fifty cheers on that disk!"

David laughed, but in a nice way. "Oh, don't feel bad. That kind of thing happens to the best of us now and then. Just be glad you didn't do it to the disk with your mailing list on it."

That didn't make me feel much better. I was mad at myself for making such a stupid mistake. I was mad at David for not warning me about it. I was mad at Mom for not being home when I needed her. Most of all, I was mad at cheerleaders who didn't have broken ankles to ruin their lives.

I went to my bedroom and got in bed. I pulled up the covers and cried myself to sleep.

"Charlie!" Mom was home.

I kept my eyes closed.

"Charlie, why didn't you get dinner ready?" she called. Silence. "Are you asleep?"

I didn't answer. I heard Dad come home. Then I must have fallen asleep again.

By ten o'clock I was awake and staring at the picture on the wall. It was the one of the new varsity cheerleading squad taken last spring. It was before everything in my life went wrong.

I heard a knock at my door. Dad came in. "Charlie, what's the problem?" he asked.

"Everything," I mumbled.

"You want to talk about it?" he asked. Dad sat down in my rocking chair.

"You know what's wrong! This dumb cast and no cheerleading and no boyfriend is what's wrong! This is the absolute *worst* summer of my life," I cried.

Dad tried to make me feel better. "Oh, I don't think it's quite that bad," he said. "You did a good job on my mailing list . . . "

"Oh, sure! And today I erased two days of work," I muttered. I turned over and smashed my face into the pillow.

"Charlie. I've had about enough of this,"

Dad said in a hard voice. "You're feeling sorry for yourself. I admit, you've had a few tough breaks this summer. But that's part of life, so grow up."

I heard Dad stand up and go over to the door. "But you don't know what I'm going through!" I sobbed.

"I think I do," Dad said. He walked over to my bed. "I went out for football in high school, you know," he said softly. "It wasn't so different then. The football players were the most popular at our school, as well as the cheerleaders," he said, smoothing back my hair.

"What happened, then?" I asked. "You didn't break *your* ankle."

"No, Charlie," Dad said quietly. "I never made the team at all."

Twelve

MOM and Dad took me out for breakfast on Saturday morning. Then I came home and started typing cheers into the computer again.

By the time David came over, I was almost finished. He showed me how to use the word processing program so that I could put the cheers into alphabetical order.

"That way it will be easier for the cheerleaders to find each cheer," he said.

Mom came over to look at our work. "Why, this is wonderful, Charlie!" she said. "What a useful idea." She looked over the printed copy of the cheers.

"Maybe you could make a copy of this for each cheerleader," she suggested. She looked up quickly to see if I was hurt by her remark. "And one for you, too, of course."

"It's okay, Mom," I said. "I know I'm not a cheerleader any more. I've just got to accept it."

Mom and Dad left to pick up some ice

cream for us. I went over to the couch and sat down. I leaned my crutches against the couch. David came over and sat next to me . . . *right* next to me.

"You're doing real well with the computer, Charlie," he said. "You should take a class in it next year."

"Maybe I will. I might not be able to take gym," I said. I moved my cast so that my leg was more comfortable. David put his arm on the back of the couch.

"You're a smart girl, Charlie. I like talking to you. I like you . . . a lot." David's arm went around my shoulders. His face was next to mine.

David closed his eyes, then he kissed me. His kiss was all right. But I didn't feel like I did when Scott kissed me. Maybe if I closed my eyes . . . and thought about Scott . . . I kissed David back. Both his arms went around me.

CRASH! My crutches fell over against the end table and knocked off some magazines. David laughed a little nervously and picked everything up.

I got up and reached out for my crutches. But David came over and started to kiss me again.

"Don't, David. It isn't going to work," I said.

"What do you mean? I know you like me,"

David said, looking hurt.

"I do like you," I answered, "as a friend. Anything else will have to wait." I couldn't think of the right way to put it. "I—I'm not over my last boyfriend yet."

"Who? That guy with the motorbike?" David asked. "Well, he's over you. I've seen him at the pool with that other cheerleader lots of times."

Mom and Dad walked in just then. They could see that things were tense. We had our ice cream and then David left. He wasn't smiling and neither was I.

I think Mom and Dad guessed what had happened. They didn't ask me to explain.

I told Lisa about it the next day when I called her.

"He's right about Scott," she said. "I've seen him with Pam at the pool and riding on his motorbike. He won't talk to me about it though."

"Maybe we could figure out some perfect boyfriends with my computer," I suggested. "Let's see, tall, dark, handsome, smart, rich . . . What else?"

"I know," Lisa started. "My sister went to a computer dance in college. That's how she met her husband."

"Really?" I liked that idea. "How did the dance work?" I asked.

"I don't know," Lisa said. "I can ask her."

Lisa came over later to tell me about the computer dance. Each person had filled out a form with his or her interests, likes and dislikes. Then a computer had matched guys with girls. Everyone was assigned a number to wear. And then they looked for matching numbers at the dance. Everyone had at least two matches.

Lisa had a fit of giggles. "My sister said one guy had thirteen girls matched with him! He must have been perfect," she said.

Mom heard us laughing and came to find out what was so funny. But she didn't laugh at the idea of a computer dance. She said it was a good idea.

"This is what we need at the Hub, girls," Mom said. "I've been trying to think of something to interest more teenagers. A computer dance! What a good idea."

"I'm not doing much dancing these days, Mom," I said.

"Well, let's see. When does that cast come off?" She looked at our calendar. "Thursday, the twenty-third, cast off," she said. "Okay, the next day is a Friday. Perfect! We'll have a back-to-school computer dance."

"I couldn't do it by myself," I said. "I don't know enough programming yet."

"But David does," Mom said. "He'll help

82

you, I'm sure. What do you think?"

I wasn't so sure. But a computer dance did sound like fun. Maybe I'd meet the guy of my dreams, someone just like Scott.

I went to David's computer class early on Tuesday. I waited for him outside. He always came to class early to set things up.

I told him about the computer dance idea as we got ready for class. "And the Hub would sponsor the dance," I said. "Could you do it?" I asked. Will you do it? I thought. Or are you too mad at me?

"Yes, I could do that with my data base program," he said. "But I'll need help."

"Oh, I'll help you." I reached out and touched his hand. "Please don't be mad at me. I still want to be friends . . . for now," I said.

"Okay," he said, and he gave me a little smile, ". . . for now."

David started teaching us about LOGO in class that day. LOGO is an easy computer programming language. You use a little triangle called a turtle to draw pictures on the screen. The kids really had fun with it. So did I.

"You'll have to get a LOGO program for your computer, Charlie," David said after class. "And after you learn that, I'll start teaching you BASIC. That's another programming language."

Well, at least we were still going to be

friends, I thought. And it would be good to have something extra to do in the fall after school. Lisa would be at cheerleading practice every night.

David and Lisa and I met at my house two days later to talk about the computer dance. We thought of lots of questions for each person to answer. Each question had to have four or five answers. It was a lot of work to write it all out.

We designed a sample form. Each person had to write his or her name, sex and grade. We didn't want to match seventh graders with seniors, or girls with girls!

Then we asked about favorite music, musical groups, movies, T.V. shows, books, sports, classes, fashions and hobbies. We asked for favorite colors, seasons and foods. After several hours of work we had a form with about thirty questions.

"Now who's going to type all this in her computer?" David asked. He handed me our notes.

"Okay," I said, laughing. "I get the job."

"Just don't store the disk by the telephone, okay, Charlie?" David said with a grin.

"Don't worry," I said as he left. "I learned that lesson the hard way. That's the kind I don't forget."

Thirteen

AS soon as David had left, Lisa said, "Why didn't you tell me he's so cute these days? And so smart!"

"Well, yes," I agreed. "But so is Scott. And why are you so interested in David anyway?" I had to tease her a little. "What about your true love, Larry?" Lisa's boyfriend, Larry, had been visiting his father in California for the whole summer.

"Oh, I'm getting tired of waiting around for him," Lisa said, "And he's not going to be in high school next year, either."

"I could probably fix things up for you with David for the computer dance," I teased. "I have connections in high places at the Hub, you know."

"Oh, stop it," Lisa said, laughing, "or I'll hide your crutches."

I worked hard on the computer dance form that week. By the next Tuesday it was finished. I took a printed copy in to class to show to David.

"Looks excellent," he said. "Wonder if I'll meet the girl of my dreams at the dance?" I couldn't look at him when he said that. I knew what he was thinking.

David and I took the form into Mom's office. She looked it over and said she would have copies printed. Then we could start handing them out to all our friends. Mom said she would have the forms passed out all over town.

At the bottom of the form was a line that said the forms had to be turned in at the Hub by August seventeenth. That gave us only a week to input the data and make the computer match-ups. David said he'd run the sorting program on his computer and help with the input, too. If lots of kids signed up for the dance, it would be a big project.

I finished putting all the cheers on my computer that week. I checked everything carefully to make sure there were no mistakes. Then I printed out eight copies. Six copies were for the cheerleaders, one for Mrs. Mac and one for me, just to remember my days as a junior high cheerleader.

Dad brought home nine green folders from his office. Our school colors are green and white. On each folder I printed in thick blue letters: "Cheers For Evergreen Junior High Varsity Cheerleaders. Collected by Charlie Hunter."

Cheerleading practice started on Monday

the thirteenth. On Tuesday Mom took me over to the school.

"I'll be back in half an hour," Mom said. "Good luck, Honey. I know this is hard for you,"

I took the folders and a stack of computer dance forms with me. I walked slowly into the school. The doctor had said I could walk without my crutches again. But I was being very careful this time.

I could see the cheerleaders practicing as I limped down the hall. They were doing Tower of Power, my cheer.

I knew who the new cheerleader was. It was Michelle Albers, an eighth grader from the junior varsity squad. She was at the top of the pyramid, in my old place. But I knew it wasn't mine any more.

"Charlie! Great to see you!" the cheerleaders yelled, crowding around me. Mrs. Mac gave me a hug.

"I did these for you on my new computer," I said as I passed out the folders.

The girls each looked through their folders. Lisa smiled at me with encouragement. "Wow, this is great," Michelle said. "Now I can learn all these words!" We all laughed with her.

"And I want to invite you all to our back-to-school computer dance at the Hub," I said. I passed out the forms and explained the dance.

"Come and meet the guy of your dreams." I didn't even look at Pam. "You're invited to the dance, too, Mrs. Mac," I said.

We all talked for a few more minutes. Then Mrs. Mac gave the cheerleaders some stretching exercises to do. She walked out to the parking lot with me.

"Looks like you've had quite a productive summer," Mrs. Mac said, "in spite of your accident." She held the heavy door open for me. "I'm quite impressed with your computer work. Are you taking Introduction to Computers this year, Charlie?"

"I didn't sign up for it," I said. "But I don't think I'll be able to take gym class this year. I'd like to take a computer class instead."

"Why don't you and your mom stop by the office before school starts? I'm sure that can be arranged," she said. Mrs. Mac waved as Mom drove up.

"Thanks for coming by, Charlie," she said, "and for those wonderful computerized cheer folders. We'll think of you whenever we use them."

I thought of her words all the way home. It was better than being forgotten.

On Friday, Mom brought all the forms for the computer dance home with her. There were almost a hundred kids signed up for the dance! That meant ninety-seven forms to enter into the computer.

David and Lisa came over that night so we could get started on our work. David brought his data base program with him and explained the sort function to us. We had to type in each person's name and grade, then M or F for male or female, then the number of each question and a letter for each answer. The computer would assign each person a number. Then we would get a master list of all the match-ups.

We worked on inputting the forms for most of the evening. David and I took turns working. He showed Lisa how to use the computer, too. He is a good teacher, I thought, and a nice guy. If only Scott were here . . . .

Mom and Dad took us all out for pizza when we finished with the computer. I could tell by the looks Lisa gave me that she was having a good time with David. He seemed to be enjoying himself, too. Maybe he wouldn't mind just being friends with me, after all.

I finished entering all the computer dance forms on Sunday. I took the disk to David on Tuesday at his class. It was our last computer class of the summer.

David had a big grin on his face when I walked in. "Guess what?" he asked. "I just had a meeting with your mom and the director of the Hub. They want me to teach two computer classes for kids this fall. And they're going to pay me!"

The kids from the class burst out laughing. "Pay you for teaching us little kids?" one boy asked. All the kids liked David and respected him, too.

"So all of you sign up for my class this fall," David said when class was over. "I'm counting on you to help me earn my spending money."

"I'll come to your new class, David," I said as we walked out.

"Good. Keep on like you're going and you'll be able to teach a class yourself by next summer," he said, smiling at me. He had the smile of a friend.

"I think Lisa should sign up for my class, too, don't you?" he asked.

"Well, yes, I think she'd enjoy it," I answered. "Why don't you ask her?"

David smiled at me again. "I think I will," he said.

Fourteen

I went to the doctor on Thursday for final X rays. Dr. Baum was there again, with his end-of-summer tan and handsome grin.

"Your X rays look okay again, Charlie," he said. "You must have been following doctor's orders this time."

I knew what to expect this time when he cut off my cast. I was just happy to be rid of it, even if my leg was white and skinny! I could always hide that with some new jeans.

I admitted I had been more careful. "And I quit cheerleading, too, like you suggested," I said.

"That must have been hard for you," the doctor said as he checked my ankle.

"It was," I said flatly. "But I have a computer now. I'm spending a lot of time with that."

"Hey, great!" Dr. Baum said. "We use a computer here in the office for our billing. And I use mine at home a lot. I have a medical update service that comes on disk every month."

"We're having a computer dance at the Hub tomorrow night," I told him. "My friends and I programmed it."

"Dancing!" Dr. Baum said, pretending to be horrified. "On the first day out of your cast?" He smiled at Mom and winked at me. Dr. Baum, Burt Reynolds' look-alike, actually winked at me! I couldn't wait to tell Lisa.

"Seriously, Charlie, I'd rather you waited two weeks or so before you try any dancing," he said. "And no gym class or athletics during fall semester, okay?"

"Okay," I agreed reluctantly. I didn't want to spend the whole computer dance sitting down. But I certainly didn't want to take a chance on hurting my ankle again, either.

"But keep up with your computer work," Dr. Baum said, smiling. "That might pay off for you in the long run much better than cheerleading."

Mom made my next doctor's appointment before we left the office. I didn't have to go back again until December.

I talked Mom into stopping at the mall on the way home. I bought some new striped jeans and a green shirt. I used some of my money from the computer work I did for Dad. Mom bought me a new pair of shoes.

"But I don't want you dancing in these tomorrow night, Charlie," she warned me. "Remember what Dr. Baum said."

"Don't worry. I'll just sit and watch," I promised.

On Friday, Lisa, David, and I met at the Hub early to get ready for the dance. We made name tags for everyone with a number next to each name. David had made a big chart with everyone's name and number and the matching numbers. But he wouldn't let us see who we were matched with.

"Why can't we see?" Lisa pleaded. "We planned this, too, you know."

"Too bad," David said, teasing her. "I'm the head programmer here. You'll just have to wait and see." And he never did let us see the chart before the dance started.

Lisa and I were getting the tape player and speakers ready. I started thinking about Scott again.

"Lisa, do you think Scott and Pam will be here?" I asked. I hated to see them together.

"I don't know," she said. "I gave his mom a form for him. He had gone camping with his friend Mark."

The kids started arriving at seven-thirty. David put up his big chart on the far side of the room. Lisa and I gave out name tags and explained how the computer matching worked.

It was eight o'clock before I could go over to look at the chart. I put on my own name tag. My number was fourteen, my fourteenth summer, I thought.

There were too many kids crowded around the chart for me to see. And I didn't want anyone to step on my ankle. When I turned around I found myself looking straight into the blue eyes I'd been thinking about all summer.

"Hi, Charlie," Scott said seriously.

"Hi," I whispered.

"So *you're* number fourteen," he said. "I've been looking all over for you. For some reason I was only matched up with one person."

David! He must have planned this for me, I thought. And that's why he wouldn't let us see the chart before the dance.

Scott put his hand on my waist and we went over to get some lemonade. I didn't know what to say.

"Are you here by yourself?" I started. Scott nodded. "Pam . . . ?" My voice trailed off.

"Oh, Pam," he said. "It was okay to teach her how to dive. And she liked riding on my motorbike. She's going with a senior now." He paused. "What about . . . ?" Scott nodded his head toward David. Lisa and David were laughing together at the computer match-up chart. David had his arm around Lisa.

"He seems pretty interested in your

cousin," I told Scott. "David taught me a lot about computers this summer. But that's all." That wasn't all he'd taught me, really. He'd taught me something about friendship. But I didn't have to tell Scott that.

We sat down on a bench along the wall. Scott reached over and took my hand. "Maybe this fall I should teach you about diving," he said. "And you can teach me about your computer. Lisa told me you're pretty good at it."

"I'd like that," I said, smiling at him. "Oh, Scott . . . "

"I missed you, Charlie," he said at the same moment. Then he reached over and kissed me on the cheek.

"I guess I felt guilty about the accident," he said, looking away. "Then your letter made me feel so bad . . . ."

I was surprised. "I didn't mean it to . . . " My words were stopped by a kiss.

"Did Lisa tell you I had quit cheerleading?" I asked him.

"I heard about it," he said. Scott put his arm around me. "It's tough for you. But actually I'm kind of glad."

"Glad?" I echoed, pulling away from him. "Why?"

"Because now you can come to the high school football games with me," he said, his blue eyes twinkling.

I smiled and shook my head. "I still have my school to support, you know. I'm not in high school yet."

"Oh, that's okay," Scott said. He took my hand again. "I'll come to some of your games with you. But I'd rather sit in the stands with you than watch you cheer."

I smiled at Scott and looked into those blue eyes. Then I leaned over and kissed him on the cheek.

"Are you allowed to dance on that ankle yet?" Scott asked.

"Nope. I'm supposed to sit right here on the sidelines," I answered.

"Well, then I guess I'll stay here with you," he said.

I decided it might not be so bad to be on the sidelines after all . . . for now. It all depended on who was there with you.